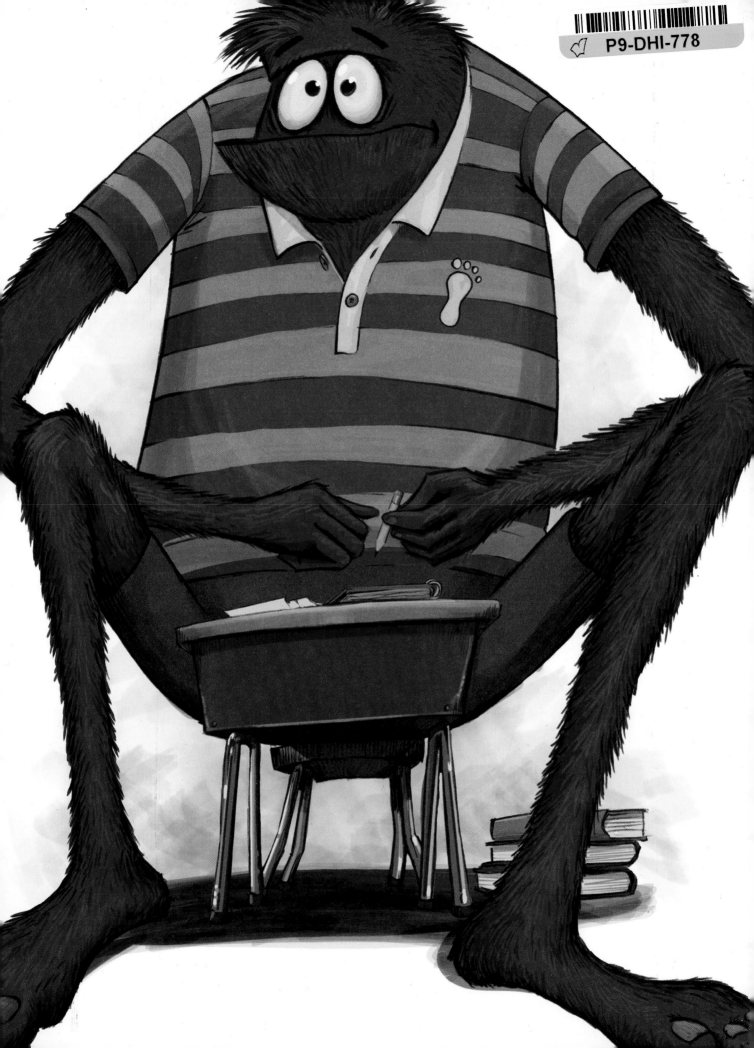

BACK
SCHOOL
BIGF

By Samantha Berger and Marth

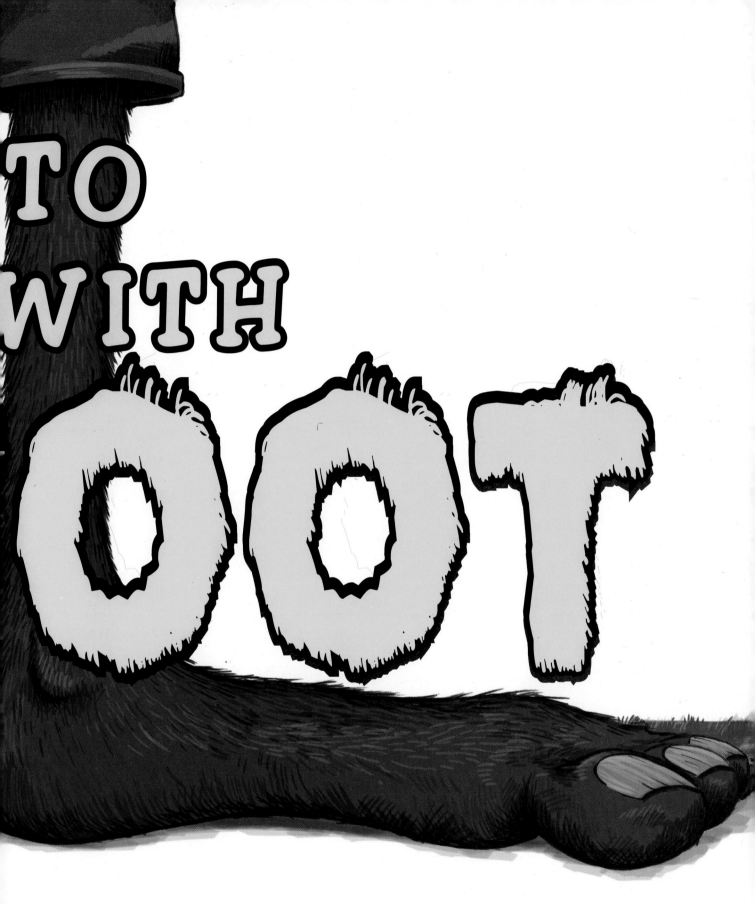

TO WITH OOT

rockenbrough · Illustrated by Dave Pressler

Scholastic Inc.

For Lin Oliver & Steve Mooser, SCBWI LEGENDS. — SB & MB

For the two art teachers in my life, my dad and
David Runnion from Deer Creek Jr. High. — DP

ISBN 978-1-338-21750-6

10 9 8 7 6 5 4 3 2 1   17 18 19 20 21

Printed in the U.S.A. 40

First printing 2017

Book design by Charles Kreloff and Steve Ponzo

The artwork for the planning stages and final color art
was created on a Wacom Cintiq using Adobe Photoshop
CC 2017. Finished line art was drawn exclusively with
Staedtler Mars Lumograph 3B Pencils on Strathmore Bristol Paper.

If you think YOU'VE got BIG back-to-school problems, let me tell you, mine are BIGGER!

Back-to-school shopping is an EXTRA-LARGE job!

Unfortunately, I am EXTRA-EXTRA-LARGE.

because I am
ALL HAIR!

And back-to-school SHOES?

Well, how do you think I got the name
BIGFOOT in the first place?!

My worries are **BIGGER** than that, though.

What if the bus driver doesn't SEE me when she comes to pick us up?

It could **TOTALLY** happen!

What if I can't stand still
for class pictures?
AGAIN!

What if at lunch . . .
I make a mistake?

The **BIGGEST** mistake in the history of big mistake making?

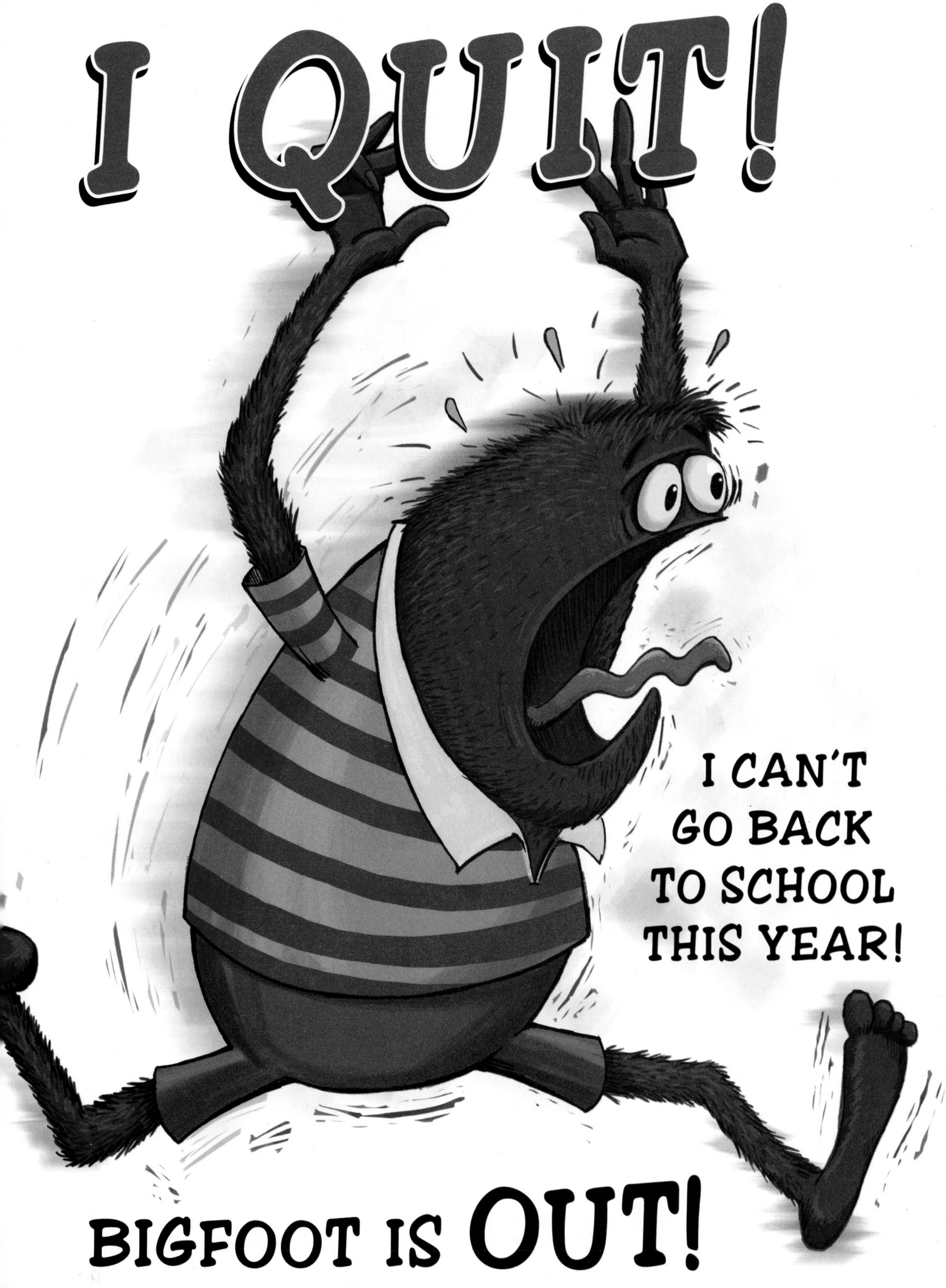
I QUIT!
I CAN'T GO BACK TO SCHOOL THIS YEAR!
BIGFOOT IS OUT!

Even if Miss Sierra Nevada is the
best teacher in our school.

Even if this is the year we get to
study mythological creatures.

Even if I won't get to see all
of my friends again.

Gulp . . . my friends.

We could do some **ENORMOUS**
art projects this year . . .

We might go on some
HUMONGOUS field trips . . .

And we will have a
TREMENDOUS
graduation ceremony at the end.

Everyone I love
will be there.

Most likely . . .

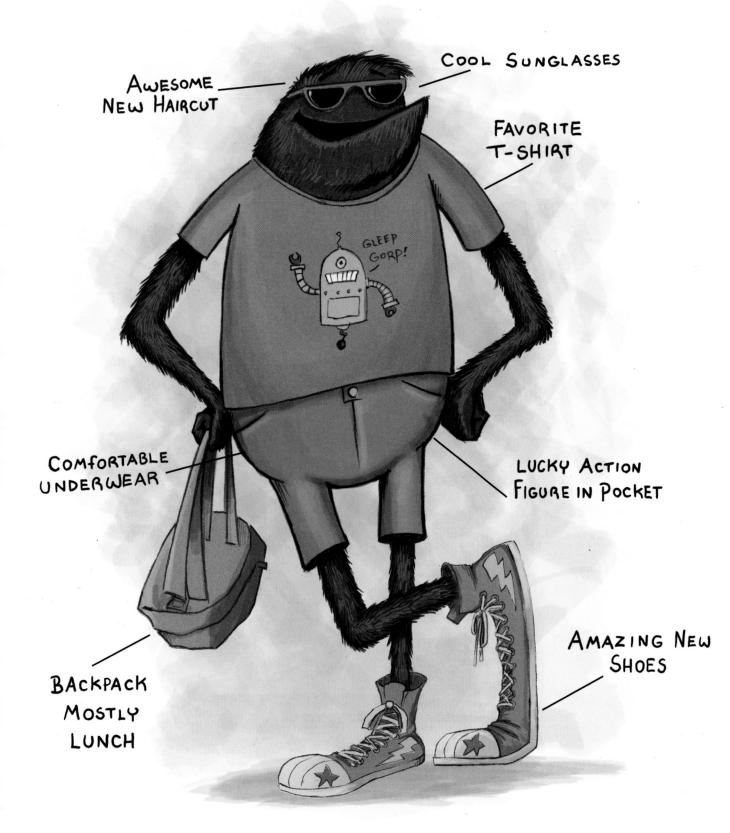

I will go back to school this year.

It's a **BIG** step, even for Bigfoot . . .